Luckiest Girl Alive by Jessica Knoll - Reviewed

By
Anthony Granger

CONTENTS

About the Author

Jessica Knoll is a new, young author getting a ton of attention for her first novel "The Luckiest Girl Alive." She has been a senior editor at Cosmopolitan Magazine and an articles editor at SELF Magazine.

She grew up in the suburbs of Philadelphia and graduated from The Shipley School in Bryn Mawr, Pennsylvania, and from Hobart and William Smith Colleges in Geneva, New York. She lives in New York City with her husband.

Themes

The themes of the novel include redemption, remorse, and the road to survival. TifAni is a complex character who tries to save her reputation through materialistic wealth and symbols of status. Her mother perpetuates the notion that wealth is gained through money and things.

In addition, TifAni struggles to show signs of remorse because she was so badly broken and taken advantage of as a child forcing her to put up a wall in order to protect herself. Yet, there's no mention of whether the classmates that were so vicious to her felt remorse for their actions until Dean pathetically apologizes.

Finally, TifAni is a survivor, but is still trying to find her path. The book highlights that just because one survives a traumatic event, it doesn't automatically mean they are healed or whole. TifAni also suffers from survivor's guilt, but avoids it by focusing on the horrible things the deceased did to her prior to their being killed.

Settings

The setting is Bryn Mawr, Pennsylvania in the suburbs of
Philadelphia where TifAni attended high school. As an adult, she
lives in Manhattan and plans to get married in Nantucket.

Short Summary

TifAni FaNelli was raised in a middle class home, but her mother always hoped she'd be able to break into the upper echelon of society so she enrolls her daughter into a private high school. TifAni is desperate to break into the popular crowd, but it leads her down a dangerous path.

Several male classmates get her drunk and rape her, but as she tries to cope with her emotions she also hopes she can remain in the popular crowd. Unfortunately, after a series of events she is cast out of the popular crowd and viciously bullied. As a result, she becomes best friends with another loner named Arthur.

Through her depression she and Arthur bond binge eating, writing nasty comments in old yearbooks, and passing notes joking about what they'd love to do to the various members of the popular group. Arthur also tells her about a previous student named Ben who tried to kill himself after being harassed by members of the popular group.

The final straw is when Arthur is expelled for sticking up for TifAni to a substitute teacher. When TifAni goes to thank him, Arthur is frustrated she never reported the sexual assault by the other students inadvertently leading to his expulsion. They get into a fight and say horrible things to each other.

Soon after, TifAni is in the lunch line when there's an explosion. A pipe bomb has gone off in the cafeteria and students scatter to seek shelter. She is with a group of students hiding under a conference room table when Ben enters and kills two of the students.

He leaves and the others try to escape, but he catches up with them and kills two more students. TifAni manages to get away and head back to the cafeteria where she finds Arthur with a rifle. He taunts her and acts as if he's going to give her the rifle to shoot one of the boys that raped her, but instead he does it. TifAni then grabs a steak knife and stabs him to death then escaped the building.

In the aftermath the boy who Arthur shot tells police that TifAni was in on the plan and she becomes a suspect as a coconspirator. Police find the old yearbook, notes, and her prints on the rifle that Arthur had previously shown her.

While the evidence is damning, they don't have enough to charge her. Public perception is that she had something to do with the shooting and she becomes a sort of local pariah, yet she never mentions the rape publicly. She returns to school with few friends and a determination to work hard and make something of herself in order to repair her damaged reputation. Marrying into a wealthy family is part of that plan.

A documentary is being made and producers want to hear her story. She doesn't plan to talk about the rape, but wants her name cleared. She also wants to reconnect with the teacher she always had a crush on.

Ultimately, through the process of filming the documentary, she comes to terms with what happened all those years ago as well as rebuild her relationship with her former teacher. In addition, she tricks the surviving boy who raped her into confessing what he did and acknowledging that he lied about her involvement in the shooting, while having his audio recorded for the documentary. She also realizes she doesn't need material wealth to redeem herself and would prefer to find someone who loves the real her. She cancels her wedding at the last minute and decides to start a new path in life that is more true to who she really is and owns her past.

Chapter 1

What Happens

TifAni and Luke are engaged planning the wedding and picking out items for their registration. TifAni is moody and never really sleeps. Luke is the ideal man who is good looking and from a prominent family with money. She works at a national magazine, but writes advice columns and articles on sex instead of the serious journalism she had hoped to do.

She is prone to panic attacks, but refers to them as "spins." She enjoys mentally unravelling people in order to determine what they want from her and then deciding whether she will play them. We learn she attended the Bradley School and that something happened there to make her infamous, even starring in an upcoming documentary.

Analysis

TifAni appears to be self-centered and materialistic. It's clear that some traumatic event has made her the way she presents herself. She is very concerned with seeming to have it all and be well put together. Her relationship with her fiancé is surface level as well. The Bradley School is foreshadowed to play a critical role in the storyline.

Study Questions

> Do you believe that something happened to TifAni when she was younger that has made it difficult for her to relate to other people?

> Why would TifAni suffer panic attacks at the thought of getting married?

Important Terms/Characters

TifAni FaNelli (Ani) – Works at *The Women's Magazine* and is engaged to Luke. She is consumed with appearances and designer brands. Something happened in her past to make her suffer from panic attacks and be somewhat cold and calculated.

Luke Harrison – He's from a wealthy and prominent New York family and is Ani's fiancé.

Nell- Ani's best friend who understands her better than anyone else. They met at Weslyan University.

Important Quotes

"She wouldn't mistake my name again, not once the documentary aired, not once the camera narrowed in on my aching, honest face, gently dissolving any last confusion about who I am and what I did." - TifAni

Chapter 2

What Happens

TifAni attended Catholic school, but was asked to leave after she and some of her friends were caught smoking pot at a friend's house. TifAni had the look of a troublemaker because of her Marilyn Monroe body type.

Her mother had TifAni take the entrance exam to get into The Bradley School in order to show up everyone at the old school and to have a better chance at an Ivy League school. TifAni was a talented writer and aced the essay portion, getting accepted and being placed in Honors English.

Analysis

Ani grew up middle class and resented her parents for her subpar and often tacky upbringing. She also often felt targeted by peers and adults because of her large chest. The Bradley School was a way to redeem her social standing.

Study Questions

1. Do Social class and social standing play a big part thus far in the story? Do you believe it will continue to play a significant role as the book continues?

Important Terms/Characters

Arthur – A student in TifAni's Honors English class who weighed close to three hundred pounds, with greasy hair, glasses, and acne. He was the first student to be kind to TifAni at her new school.

Beth (The Shark) – Another student at The Bradley School who was friends with Arthur. Her nickname was "The Shark" because her eyes were so set far apart.

Hilary – One of the popular girls at Bradley.

HOs – The nickname given to Hilary and Olivia, the most popular girls in school.

Liam – Also a new student at Bradley, he was very attractive and TifAni had a crush on him.

Mr. Larson – The Honors English teacher who was very attractive and only 10 years older than his students.

Mt. St. Theresa's – The Catholic School in Malvern, PA Ani attended until the ninth grade when she went to The Bradley School.

Olivia – One of the popular girls at Bradley.

Sarah – Another student at The Bradley School who ate lunch with TifAni, Arthur, Beth, and Teddy.

Teddy – Sarah's boyfriend who also ate lunch with TifAni, Beth, and Arthur.

The Bradley School – Located in Bryn Mawr, PA it was a private high school for the wealthy.

The Main Line – Where all of the upper class lived in Eastern Pennsylvania and where The Bradley School was situated.

Important Quotes

"It's okay to be insufferable as long as you're aware that you're being insufferable. At least that's how I justified it to myself." - TifAni

Chapter 3

What Happens

Ani is very much focused on her four carat emerald engagement ring that was her fiancé's grandmother's ring because it symbolizes status. She's also focused on making sure she wears the perfect outfit. It's learned that TifAni had seen Luke at a party and made it her goal to become his girlfriend. Her friend Nell had helped her scheme and plan.

Now they were picking out bridesmaids dresses and discussing the pedigree of Luke's family. TifAni is not only trying to lose weight for the wedding, but also apparently for a documentary in which she will be starring. The subject of the documentary is unknown to the reader, but TifAni hopes it will help clear her name.

Analysis

TifAni feels she has something to prove and uses material wealth to do so. Something in her past has made her doubt herself and she believes others judge her for it.

Study Questions

1. Do you think TifAni loves Luke or is there something else contributing to her wanting to marry him?

Chapter 4

What Happens

Her second week of school, TifAni asked her mother for a whole new wardrobe in order to fit in better at her new school. She typically hung out with Arthur and his friends while trying to get Hillary and Olivia to like her. She also joined the cross country team in order to avoid PE class. Mr. Larson was the cross country coach. Eventually she is invited to sit at the cafeteria table with Hillary and Olivia. Arthur isn't thrilled with her decision to sit with them and admits he pretty much hates everyone. Hillary and Olivia encourage

TifAni to go to the dance, but when they don't show up she runs outside to cry. Once outside, Hillary who has taken to calling TifAni "Finny" because of a suggestion from Dean, is outside and calls her over to a car with Dean, Peyton, and Olivia. They tell her they're going to "The Spot," a remote patch of land blocked off by trees to drink beer.

Peyton tells TifAni that Olivia claims to have seen Arthur giving Ben Hunter a blow job and when it got around school Ben tried to kill himself. Dean invites TifAni to a party at his house, but tells her not to mention it to Hillary and Olivia. TifAni takes a cab there and wears her sexiest underwear in case something happens with Liam.

She tells her mother she's spending the night at Hillary's house. Dean, Peyton, and Liam are there drinking heavily and playing beer pong. Tifani joins them and drinks a ton of whiskey. Next thing she knows, she's on the floor of the guest bedroom with Peyton in between her legs. She falls back asleep and awakes in pain finding Liam on top of her. She says "Ow," but it sounds more like moaning because she's so inebriated.

She passes out and awakens the next morning in bed next to Dean. She rushes around to find her clothes and takes the train home, but purposely missed her stop. She calls the school and lets them know she's missed her stop and will be late. She stops off at a Chinese buffet rather than have to go home and that's when she recalls a salty taste in her mouth and has a flashback to Dean putting himself into her mouth and groaning.

Analysis

TifAni's being raped is pivotal to the story and explains why she has become so guarded. Her desire to please and be a part of the popular group is overwhelming. Her classmates' cruel behavior ultimately puts other events that will change all of their lives into motion.

Study Questions

1. What does it say about TifAni that she is so consumed with being popular that after she puts herself in a dangerous situation?

2. Does society perceive what happened to TifAni as rape or would some think she deserved it because she was drunk?

Important Terms/Characters

Dean Barton – One of the popular boys at The Bradley School who TifAni isn't interested in, but who makes her perform oral sex on when she is blacked out.

Peyton - One of the popular boys at The Bradley School who TifAni

Important Quotes

"Life had shifted drastically while I slept, but Dean was looking at me like we were comrades in this post-party apocalypse, and it was so impossibly tempting to accept that reality over the other one that I did with a weak laugh." - TifAni

Chapter 5

What Happens

TifAni's boss LoLo has a pitch meeting and Eleanor tries to show up TifAni, but it backfires on her and TifAni's story idea is accepted. Luke would like TifAni to join him for dinner with a client and his wife. She'd put it off for a few days, but knew she had to go and play the role of the dutiful spouse. Luke introduces her to Whitney and her husband Andrew who looked familiar. She finally realizes it is her old teacher, Mr. Larson.

Once he realizes who she is, Andrew recalls what she his Honors English student. He's now married to Whitney with two children. In her mind, TifAni recalls Luke's conservative upbringing and his laissez-faire perception of Planned Parenthood who she credits with her own not having a 13 year-old child. She told him about "that night," but he doesn't want to talk about it especially on camera. Whitney asks TifAni if she's doing the documentary because Andrew has agreed to do it and she says she can't talk about it. Whitney infers that means she's also doing it.

Analysis

Reconnecting with her old teacher Andrew Larson stirs emotions in TifAni and has her thinking about past events. It also has her looking at her fiancé more critically because he doesn't really understand her or what she's been through.

Study Questions

1. Do you believe it really was a coincidence that TifAni ran into Andrew Larson again after all these years?

2. Why is Luke such a contradiction to everything Tifani believes in and yet she continues to want to marry him?

Important Terms/Characters

LoLo – TifAni's boss at *The Women's* Magazine who is trying to get TifAni a position with the New York Times Magazine.

Eleanor – TifAni's coworker at *The Women's Magazine* who is always trying to one up TifAni especially since she recently planned a lavish wedding of her own.

Important Quotes

"It doesn't affect you, it doesn't affect me. What does affect you and me though? Obama taxing the shit out of us because we're in the highest bracket." – Luke

"That other stuff does affect me, though." – Ani

"You're on birth control!" What do you need an abortion for?" – Luke

"Luke, if it weren't for Planned Parenthood I could have a thirteen year-old right now." – Ani

"I'm not doing now." – Luke

Chapter 6

What Happens

It's the morning after Dean's party and TifAni is driving around in
Dean's car with Liam and two sophomores from the soccer team.
Earlier that morning she told him she didn't know how she ended
up in Dean's room and he told her that he didn't care that she has
hooked up with him too. They go to a diner for breakfast and
TifAni is nauseous the entire time thinking about what had
occurred the night before and the possible consequences of being
pregnant. She obsessively drinks water to deal with the anxiety,
something that continues today.

Finally her mother comes to pick her up believing she has spent the
night at Olivia's house. TifAni is short with her and ends up
grounded. Before they can make it home, TifAni vomits in her
hand. For the rest of the weekend she throws up nonstop and
barely sleeps. At school on Monday it was clear everyone had
heard.

The Shark acted concerned for her and after class Mr. Larson asks
her to stay so that he can see if she is ok, having heard all the
rumors. He encourages her to see the school nurse, but she says she
has it under control. To her surprise, she was still welcomed at the
HOs lunch table thanks to Dean's influence, but there was still
tension. Before leaving the cafeteria TifAni catches up with Liam
and tactfully questions whether he used a condom.

He doesn't respond, but says she only has a 23% chance of getting
pregnant making no sense. She tells him she still plans to go to
Planned Parenthood for the morning after pill. She told him she
knew of one not too far away and he told her he'd secure
transportation for after school. They go together and TifAni gets
several pills, but when TifAni leaves the doctor's office Liam isn't
in the waiting room. She panics, but sees that he's waiting outside.

Analysis

Following the rape, TifAni doesn't know how to decipher her
emotions. She's physically ill and lashes out at her mother, but

tries to appease the boys who took advantage of her and not make waves within the popular group. She's smart to get the morning after pill, but yet she refuses help from peers and her teacher. She's willing to do whatever it takes to make things go back to the way they used to be.

Study Questions

1. Is TifAni trying to put the rape out of her mind in order to remain popular or could there be more going on there in terms of avoidance?

2. Do you think teenage boys educated on protected sex and what constitutes rape?

Important Quotes

"I would have welcomed some crazy's bomb going off in that moment. One last tragedy that would anchor Liam to me. I pictured him rushing me, covering my body with his as fiery shards of building sphered through the air. No screams at first, everyone too stunned, too singularly focused on just surviving. That would be the most surprising lesson I'd learn at Bradley: You only scream when you're finally safe." - TifAni

Chapter 7

What Happens

TifAni's mom is infatuated with the Harrison's and their lavish lifestyle and enjoys all of the wedding planning while TifAni gets frustrated with her lack of class. TifAni and Luke hang out with his friend Bailey and TifAni becomes angry with how Luke treats his friend. He becomes bossy and demeaning and she confronts him about his behavior.

She feels that his treating his friend that way is his being an elitist and makes her also feel like a second class citizen. Luke is also irritating at times and downplays what has happened to her in the past. It doesn't help that she's not eating in order to be in top shape for the wedding.

Luke's cousin Hallsy visits them at the Harrison Nantucket home bringing pot brownies she got from "the help." TifAni has a brownie and unfortunately makes a snide comment to Hallsy after she makes a racist remark that upsets Luke because he thinks she should have just let it go. They fight and Luke sleeps in the guest house, but the following morning TifAni apologizes.

Analysis

TifAni's agitation with Luke is growing as the wedding nears because she knows he's not right for her. In addition, she frequently self-sabotages the good things in her life.

Study Questions

1. Does TifAni even like the person Luke is or is she just marrying him for his reputation?

Important Quotes

"Come on, you're a survivor." – Luke

"This is Luke's favorite thing to say to me. I'm a survivor. It's the finality of the word that bothers me, its assuming implication. Survivors should move on. Should wear white wedding dresses and carry peonies down the aisle and overcome, rather than dwell in a past that can't be altered. The word dismisses something I cannot, will not, dismiss.

Chapter 8
What Happens

It's becoming clear that Liam is interested in Olivia, but TifAni won't cause any waves in order to remain in the group. Hilary invited TifAni over for a sleepover at Olivia's house. They started drinking and then Olivia suggests they invite Dean over. Both Liam and Dean come once it's dark. After more drinking they go outside to smoke pot. The others slipped away claiming they had to go to the bathroom.

TifAni tries to get Dean to go inside, but instead he kisses her. She continues to try, but Dean grabs her by the pants making her fall backward and landing in her wrist. He yells at her to "Shut up" and slaps her. He begins unbuttoning her pants when Olivia's father starts yelling and Olivia runs out of the house telling them to leave.

Dean and the others ran for the car while TifAni walked in the other direction. She walked until she found a gas station to ask for directions to the train. The cashier is concerned about TifAni, but she doesn't want him to contact the police. Another customer enters and it turns out to be Mr. Larson who offers to take her home.

Once in his car, she falls apart crying, telling him everything that happened. He took her back to his apartment, gave her frozen pizza, and put her to bed. She has nightmares and asks him to sleep in the same room with her so he sleeps on the floor and stays awake listening to his breathing.

The next morning while Mr. Larson is out getting a bandage for her face, TifAni calls her mother. TifAni takes the opportunity to call her mother who says Dean called looking for her. She calls Dean and he says they were all worried about her so she lies and says she stayed with a cross country teammate.

Dean apologizes for hitting her and begs her not to tell anyone. She reluctantly agrees. She calls her mother back and tells her she plans on taking the train home and mentions that Olivia's dog scratched her face. TifAni asks Mr. Larson to take her to the train station, which he does reluctantly.

Analysis

TifAni continues to get into situations she can't control that end up with her being taken advantage of. Dean is manipulative and can't control his rage making TifAni an easy target and a victim of abuse again.

Study Questions

1. Why do you think Hilary and Olivia wanted to invite Dean over in the first place?

Important Quotes

"All my life, I've found it difficult to advocate for myself, to ask for what I want. I fear burdening people so much. I'd like to blame it on what happened that night, on what happened in the ensuing weeks, but I think it's just part of my blueprint." - TifAni

Chapter 9

What Happens

TifAni tells Luke she plans to e-mail Mr. Larson. She doesn't mention that she's fantasizing about kissing him. After some negotiating via e-mail Mr. Larson agrees to meet her for drinks. They chit chat, flirt, and talk about the documentary. When he gets a call from his wife, but doesn't answer, TifAni finally tells him she's sorry for what happened so long ago in the headmaster's office.

She admits that she didn't come forward about what Dean had done to her because she had spoken to him on the phone when Mr. Larson had run to CVS for bandages and she was concerned about no longer being popular. He tells her there's nothing to apologize for that he understands. They agree to meet again when they are back in Pennsylvania for the documentary.

Analysis

TifAni has always had strong feelings for her former teacher and hopes to explore them without his wife around. She feels a strong connection to him and he can relate to her past experiences unlike her fiancé.

Study Questions

1. Do you feel TifAni's reaching out to her former teacher is another way to sabotage her wedding?

Important Quotes

"I may never fully make my way out of the bourgey pit, but that doesn't mean I'm not a trophy wife too. I'm just a different kind." - TifAni

Chapter 10
What Happens

TifAni finds Olivia and apologizes for getting her in trouble with her dad. She tells her not to worry about it, but also has a cut on her cheek. Dean comes to the table and he's angry that he was called to the headmaster's office. She tries to tell him she didn't say anything, but he says they had to find out he was involved somehow. He yells at her to leave their table and Olivia, Liam, and Peyton smirk.

It didn't help that when leaving the cafeteria she saw the plaque Barton Family, 1998. After cross country practice she decides to take a shower since her mother is picking her up to go shopping and as she goes to get dressed she runs into Olivia and Hilary in the locker room. When she spots them they say they were looking for her to see what she was doing that night and she's relieved, but tells them she has to go shopping with her mother.

While waiting for her mother, Arthur sits on the curb to see if she's ok. They hadn't spoken since she had started hanging out with the popular crowd, but her mother pulls up and she has to go. The next morning TifAni is surprised that everyone is laughing and staring at her. She comes to realize her cross country shorts stained from finally getting her period had been stolen out of the locker room by Olivia and Hilary and hung in the seniors lounge with a sign that said "Sniff a Skank." She cries in the bathroom and then decides to skip school and on the way out runs into Arthur who convinces her to come to his house.

Arthur eats and hands her back her dirty shorts he took from the lounge. She cries and then he takes her to the basement to show her an old yearbook and to explain that he and Dean had been best friends just a few years ago before he had a growth spurt. He closes the yearbook and shows her a rifle that was his father's before he left his mother. He gives it to hold and promises it's not loaded.

After that, for the next several weeks, she runs the first mile of cross country practice then runs over to Arthur's house where they binge eat and write nasty comments alongside photos in the old yearbook before she returns to cross country or heads home on the train. They smoked pot and Arthur also told her why Ben really tried to kill himself.

Apparently Dean had pretended to be his friend then with a group of guys held him down and taken a shit on his chest. During those weeks of hanging out, Mr. Larson also left the school without any explanation. A substitute, Mrs. Hurst, took his place. She has heard the rumors about TifAni and treated her horribly.

When she was particularly cruel to TifAni in front of the class Arthur got in her face and defended TifAni, which got him expelled because he has previously been suspended for an outburst in Biology class that had been a dare by Dean.

She goes to his house and demands he let her in so that they can talk, but they get into a heated argument because he's frustrated that he got expelled and TifAni continues to protect Dean. TifAni lashes out and grabs the framed photo of Arthur and his dad, which is the most precious to him, and runs out of the house to the train.

Analysis

Arthur's being expelled is a key plot turn within the novel. It sets into motion a set of events that change all of the characters trajectories.

Study Questions

1. Why is it significant that Arthur shows TifAni his father's rifle?

2. Why would Arthur tell TifAni about what happened to Ben?

Important Terms/Characters

Mrs. Hurst – A substitute teacher that is nasty to TifAni because of the rumors circulating.

Important Quotes

"You should be mad at you! You had the chance to take him down and you didn't because you actually thought you could redeem yourself." - Arthur

Chapter 11

What Happens

TifAni receives an e-mail offering her a Features Director at a smaller magazine. It would be a promotion, but with less prestige so she puts it out of her mind. She meets Nell for dinner, but barely eats because she's still dieting for the wedding. Nell gives her a hard time and TifAni admits she's not sure if marrying Luke is the right thing to do, but she does love him. TifAni doesn't mention she's only marrying Luke for the redemption marrying a Harrison could bring. Nell doesn't buy it and tells her it's not too late to cancel the wedding.

They get into a big fight. A few weeks pass and TifAni heads to Pennsylvania for the documentary production. She makes sure the director books her a hotel room so that she doesn't have to stay with her parents.

She sits on a stool with a black background and he tells her to say her name (she uses her married name since the documentary will air in a few months) and how old she was on November 12, 2001. Then, he asks her to tell her story and says that it's ok if she has to cry. She doesn't feel emotional, but does feel nauseous.

Analysis

TifAni's starving herself in order to look great on her wedding day is another way for her to focus on a pain unrelated to her past. Her friend Nell sees it and just wants to help, but TifAni isn't ready. Filming the documentary could explain what happened to make her the way she is today.

Study Questions

1. Is TifAni starving herself simply to look good in a wedding dress?

2. The documentary mentions a specific date, could it not be about the rape?

Important Terms/Characters

Aaron – The director of the documentary who gets TifAni to tell her story.

Chapter 12
What Happens

They were in the cafeteria and both Dean and TifAni were in line
for the cashier, but she chose the line farther away from Olivia and
Hilary's table. Next thing she knows Dean is jumping and she
smells smoke while she lands on the ground. Teddy takes her and
pulls her out of the cafeteria. They can't get out of the building the
way they came in so they go upstairs to the Baulkin Room, a
conference room.

She'd be told later that Hilary lay on the floor of the cafeteria
missing a foot and Olivia was dead. They hide under the
conference table with another student named Ansilee, Liam, The
Shark, and Peyton. Someone with a semiautomatic handgun walks
in seconds later and peeks under the table.

Ansilee takes off running and he shoots her in the back. He peeks
back under the table and The Shark tries to talk Ben down since
she had been friends with him. Peyton also tried so Ben shot him in
the face. Then, he walked out of the room. None of them had a
cellphone because there hadn't been time to grab their backpack.
Smoke was coming in from the cafeteria and they couldn't get the
window open so they had to leave the room. Peyton moans and
was still breathing, but he was too heavy for them to carry.

Teddy makes the call to go upstairs to where the old boarding
rooms are when he's shot in his collarbone. Everyone else takes off
running downstairs. At the end of the stairs Liam runs right to seek
shelter in an empty classroom and TifAni and The Shark turn left
so as to not be cornered. Ben followed Liam into the classroom
and shot him. TifAni and The Shark headed back to the newer part
of the cafeteria where sprinklers had gone off and ankle deep water
had gathered. Blocking the exit was Arthur with his father's rifle
surrounded by bodies and damage from the blast.

Dean was slumped over the cash register with one side of his body
burned. Arthur tells The Shark to leave and she runs out of the
building past him. Arthur pointed the rifle at TifAni and said she
was sorry for taking the photo and begged him to not shoot her.

He instead tells her to take the gone so she can shoot Dean's penis off and goes to hand her the gun. She reaches for it in order to save herself and he takes the gun back shooting Dean between the legs. She then begins stabbing Arthur with a steak knife and that's when he says he was just trying to help her. She ends the story there for the director silently recalling how she had hoped killing Arthur would somehow redeem her with the popular crowd.

Analysis

The shooting at the school changes everything for all the characters as their lives will never be the same. The scars from that day are both physical and mental for all impacted by the violence.

Study Questions

1. Why would Arthur offer to give the gun to TifAni and do you believe he sincerely was trying to help her?

Important Quotes

"My mom always told me to never fight off a rapist with a knife," I said so woozy from the heat it didn't even occur to me the morbid hilarity of saying that to Liam. - TifAni

Chapter 13
What Happens

The director called cut and told everyone go out for drinks. He reminds TifAni that she has an early call the next morning and asks her if she wouldn't mind doing something during the shoot that isn't revealed to the reader, but she agrees. She emails Andrew to see if he'll meet her for pizza now rather than waiting until the following day to meet up.

She doesn't hear from him and uses some liquid courage to call his parents' home where she assumes he's staying. He answers and agrees to meet her. Once together she admits it was hard to tell her story to the film crew and was concerned about whether people would believe her. She admits to getting hate mail from Dean's supporters, but both her mom and Luke don't want her to mention the sexual abuse on camera.

She's also hesitant to mention Liam's rape since he died in the shooting. They decide to break into The Bradley School and find the door to the Athletic Complex is unlocked. They reminisce and Andrew lets TifAni know he was forced to leave because Dean's parents forced him out when he pushed the TifAni incident. TifAni recalled returning to school after the shooting and how she became close friends with The Shark. They both admit to thinking about Arthur often and TifAni says she doesn't feel bad about killing him and fears she's a cold, selfish person. Andrew assures her that she's not and that she's the bravest person he knows.

Once in his old classroom and Andrew admits it wasn't a coincidence that they reconnected at dinner through Luke. He had looked her up and pushed for Luke to set up the meeting so that he could see her again. A security man enters the building and they hide under the teacher's desk, but once he's left Andrew can't get TifAni out from under the desk because she's having a panic attack. He apologizes once he realizes what he's done and finally lifts her out and hold her up then they kiss.

Analysis

Going back to The Bradley School with her former teacher was sure to stir up emotions, but the hiding under the desk brought to the surface TifAni hadn't yet faced. Having Mr. Larson there for comfort is translated into a romantic scenario.

Study Questions

1. Should TifAni and Mr. Larson become romantically involved?

2. Is Mr. Larson the only person who can identify with what TifAni has been through?

Important Quotes

"I can stab my friend to death, but I can't admit I'm about to marry the wrong guy." - TifAni

Chapter 14
What Happens

TifAni recalls the immediate aftermath of the shooting from waking up in the hospital to going home. She's questioned by detectives as well as a forensic psychologist. Ansilee, Olivia, Teddy, Liam, and Peyton were all dead. Ben had also killed himself. Dean probably won't be able to walk again. TifAni is focused on returning to Bradley no matter what the cost. Once home, her mother doesn't want her to watch the news, but she sneaks a peak anyway and learns about Hilary losing her foot. Her mom gives her a sleeping pill recommended by the psychologist.

Mr. Larson had called to check up on her, but her mother wouldn't let her speak with him. Detectives ask TifAni to come down to the station to answer more questions so her mother gets her a lawyer, Daniel Rosenberg. TifAni is asked to confide in the lawyer so she tells him everything. When she mentions that she has seen and held Arthur's rifle when he first showed it to her at his house he grows worried and then separately tells her parents the police could have her prints on the gun.

The two detectives that previously questioned her ask her about the yearbook and nasty comments they found in it. They also have notes she and Arthur passes saying they'd love to kill them all and Arthur reminds her he has his father's gun. TifAni maintains she thought he was joking. Before leaving,

 Dan tells TifAni that if she doesn't tell her parents about the rape he will. The next day he calls and TifAni overhears him telling her mother everything. Her mother is furious with TifAni for putting herself in the situation to begin with and blames her for the rape. TifAni and her mother attend Liam's funeral and no one wants to sit in the same pew. TifAni promised herself she'd work hard to succeed since Liam no longer had a chance.

The school was surprised when her mother told them she was returning, but there wasn't enough evidence to charge her with a crime despite Dean telling them that Arthur handed her the gun and told her to shoot him just like "they had planned." The school was also worried about a lawsuit and already had one from Peyton's parents because the sprinkler system hadn't worked on one side of the cafeteria and Peyton dies from the smoke, not the bullet.

Ironically, Dean became an inspirational speaker after attending boarding school. Hilary also moved away to Illinois. TifAni saw living a luxurious life as a way to redeem herself and to not be hurt again.

Analysis

TifAni's need to return to the same school appears to be a way to avoid reality rather than face the situation head on. It's also a means to rebuild her reputation, which is important to her.

Study Questions

1. After a traumatic event like the school shooting, do you feel it makes sense people would want to blame someone that is still alive like TifAni?

2. Why is it so important for TifAni to return to The Bradley School?

Important Terms/Characters

Daniel Rosenberg – TifAni's lawyer who believes she is a suspect.

Chapter 15
What Happens

TifAni was convinced by the director to visit Arthur's mother who often wrote TifAni letters and cards. They look through photo albums together and Mrs. Finnerman says she doesn't believe her boy could have been a psychopath like the media portrayed him to be. TifAni didn't say it, but she did believe Arthur was a psychopath that happened to have genuine feelings for her. Ben was depressed and suicidal making him the perfect partner for Arthur.

Arthur had wanted to kill anyone he felt was intellectually inferior to him while Ben just wanted to seek revenge. Arthur had been responsible for the pipe bombs and getting Ben onboard. TifAni admits to Mrs. Finnerman she has the photo of Arthur and his father and promises to return it to her. The meeting is cut short when Mrs. Finnerman gets a migraine and is unable to continue.

After kissing in the classroom apparently TifAni and Andrew had gone back to his parents' house drank and made out on his bed, but TifAni was feverish so he tucked her in and she slept for the first time in a very long time. After leaving Mrs. Finnerman's house TifAni canceled plans to eat with her mother at the local fancy Chinese restaurant, but when she showed up to meet Andrew there her mother and aunt were dining because Luke had offered to pay.

TifAni lied and said she was simply picking up a to-go order, but they insist she eat with them. Acting like she's going to the bathroom, she meets Andrew outside and explains her mother is in the restaurant. He thinks maybe it's for the best that they don't take things any further, but TifAni grows frustrated and upset picking a fight because she's hurt. She returns to eat with her mother and aunt, but is short with both of them.

After paying the bill she heads to her car and pretends not to notice Andrew's car still in the parking lot. He pulls away once she's inside her own car. The Spot had been turned into a nice park and TifAni reluctantly meets up with Dean and the documentary crew. He's in a wheelchair and wants to set the record straight, but when she mentions the assault he asks the production crew to give them some privacy.

Once alone, she gets Dean to admit that he and the others raped her and that if Olivia's dad hadn't interrupted them he probably would have raped her again. He's willing to say on camera that she had nothing to do with Arthur's plan and that he made that up because he was angry, but not mention the assault because he now has a reputation to preserve. Aaron comes back because they're losing daylight and they finish the take. TifAni only feels slightly guilty knowing had Arthur given her the rifle she may have actually shot Dean.

Analysis

While both TifAni and Mr. Larson feel a connection, they missed their chance long ago. He helps her to begin to heal, but she needs to find herself before she can commit to a relationship and he is committed to his family.

Study Questions

1. Is it best that TifAni and Mr. Larson don't have a sexual relationship?

2. Why do they feel so connected to each other?

Chapter 16

What Happens

TifAni returns to New York and while she tries to convince Luke to let the production crew film their wedding he works to convince her to move to London for a promotion he's been offered. She tells him she met with Dean and she locates the folder she had been storing the photo of Arthur in on a bookshelf. Luke tells her she probably moved it when she can't find the frame. A few days later she meets Nell to get her hair done for the wedding.

They then run back to her apartment to gather her luggage and throw out the trash prior to leaving for Nantucket. As they hurry around TifAni goes to grab a trash bag and something falls out from under the sink. Luke's brother gives a toast at the rehearsal dinner and TifAni and Nell are both disgusted by how little he actually knows her and how he mentions Luke dealing with her moods.

TifAni heads to the bathroom and finds in her purse part of the photo frame she had found under the kitchen sink. She begins crying and Nell comes to check on her and does what she asks. Luke comes to check on her and she confronts him about the frame.

He admits to doing cocaine with a friend and using the frame to cut the drugs, but someone knocked it over and it broke so he threw it away. He threw away the photo too so that she wouldn't know what had happened. He thought she should move on anyway from her past and not to let this ruin their night. She informs him that's not what is going to ruin the night. TifAni and Nell end up on the ferry the next morning headed back to New York.

Analysis

Luke's and TifAni's relationship is all about manipulation. In addition, Luke doesn't respect TifAni or fully understand who she is as a person. Tifani finally understands she has to end the relationship despite the consequences.

Study Questions

1. Why do you feel the broken photo frame was the last straw for TifAni?

Chapter 17

What Happens

The Harrisons were angry, but also sympathetic about TifAni's canceling the wedding while her mother was furious. TifAni was in a fog during the immediate aftermath and had to film her name again for the documentary crew since she wasn't getting married. Instead of using her made up name "Ani" she was proud to use her given name of TifAni FaNelli.

She also accepted the new job at the smaller magazine because she needed the additional funds to try to repay the Harrisons for what they had put out for the wedding. She's also more focused on finding someone that truly accepts her rather than having a big, fat emerald on her finger.

She received a phone call from Aaron and he admits she was right, both she and Dean were still had microphones on when he confessed to raping her. Dean should have realized with the number of interviews he had done, but the microphone had slipped his mind. While Aaron is hesitant to use the audio, TifAni tells him to go for it and that she's ready for the truth to come out.

Analysis

TifAni may have been vulnerable and an easy target as a child, but she has learned to fight back. By tricking Dean into confession while wearing a microphone she's taking back the power in the relationship. She's finally standing up for herself and becoming stronger.

Study Questions

1. Do you think it's fair that TifAni tricked Dean into confessing?

Important Quotes

"I just want to be sure you're prepared for the backlash – I imagine people will be pretty outraged." – Aaron

"Of course they will. It was a terrible thing they did to me." - TifAni

Critical Reviews

The novel is being compared to the smash hit thriller "Gone Girl" because of its dark and dramatic turn of events. Readers and reviewers have described it as a page turner that's addictive.

Fans enjoy the building tension and are excited that it is being made into a movie. The plot is seen as compelling and dramatic.

Other readers found TifAni to be whiny and void of human emotion and questioned the plausibility of events as well as the unsympathetic classmates.

Final Thoughts

This book was better than "Gone Girl," which plays out like a bad Lifetime movie. In my opinion, it's believable and intriguing especially as school shootings have become more prevalent in society.

TifAni is a dynamic character in which the author evolves through her past experiences that have made her the person she is today. She is jaded, but once her past is revealed it all makes sense why.

The novel is an exploration of human character and the imperfect way in which people survive traumatic events. Nothing is sugar coated and the author understands victimization can impact people differently, but there's no hiding from the past.

Glossary/Characters

Aaron – The director of the documentary who gets TifAni to tell her story.

Arthur – A student in TifAni's Honors English class who weighed close to three hundred pounds, with greasy hair, glasses, and acne. He was the first student to be kind to TifAni at her new school. He ends up plotted a school massacre.

Beth (The Shark) – Another student at The Bradley School who was friends with Arthur. Her nickname was "The Shark" because her eyes were so set far apart.

Daniel Rosenberg – TifAni's lawyer who believes she is a suspect.

Dean Barton – One of the popular boys at The Bradley School who TifAni isn't interested in, but who makes her perform oral sex on when she is blacked out and almost rapes her.

Eleanor – TifAni's coworker at *The Women's Magazine* who is always trying to one up TifAni especially since she recently planned a lavish wedding of her own.

Hilary – One of the popular girls at Bradley.

HOs – The nickname given to Hilary and Olivia, the most popular girls in school.

Liam – Also a new student at Bradley, he was very attractive and TifAni had a crush on him. He ends up raping her.

LoLo – TifAni's boss at *The Women's* Magazine who is trying to get TifAni a position with the New York Times Magazine.

Luke Harrison – He's from a wealthy and prominent New York family and is Ani's fiancé.

Mr. Andrew Larson – The Honors English teacher who was very attractive and only 10 years older than his students. He and TifAni have a special connection.

Mt. St. Theresa's – The Catholic School in Malvern, PA Ani attended until the ninth grade when she went to The Bradley School.

Nell- Ani's best friend who understands her better than anyone else. They met at Weslyan University.

Olivia – One of the popular girls at Bradley.

Peyton - One of the popular boys at The Bradley School who TifAni

Sarah – Another student at The Bradley School who ate lunch with TifAni, Arthur, Beth, and Teddy.

Teddy – Sarah's boyfriend who also ate lunch with TifAni, Beth, and Arthur.

The Bradley School – Located in Bryn Mawr, PA it was a private high school for the wealthy.

The Main Line – Where all of the upper class lived in Eastern Pennsylvania and where The Bradley School was situated.

TifAni FaNelli (Ani) – Works at *The Women's Magazine* and is engaged to Luke. She is consumed with appearances and designer brands. Something happened in her past to make her suffer from panic attacks and be somewhat cold and calculated.

Made in the USA
Las Vegas, NV
13 September 2022

55252867R00030